Overcom
Sports Biographies

Wilt Chamberlain: NBA Giant

by

Alan Venable

Don Johnston Incorporated
Volo, Illinois

2

Edited by:

Jerry Stemach, MS, CCC-SLP
Speech/Language Pathologist, Director of Content Development, Start-to-Finish Books

Gail Portnuff Venable, MS, CCC-SLP
Speech/Language Pathologist, San Francisco, California

Dorothy Tyack, MA
Learning Disabilities Specialist, San Francisco, California

Consultant:

Ted S. Hasselbring, PhD
William T. Brian Professor of Special Education Technology, University of Kentucky

Graphics and Illustrations:

Photographs and illustrations are all created professionally and modified to provide the best possible support for the intended reader.

Narration:

Professional actors and actresses read the text to build excitement and to model research-based elements of fluency: intonation, stress, prosody, phrase groupings and rate. The rate has been set to maximize comprehension for the reader.

Published by:

Don Johnston Incorporated
26799 West Commerce Drive
Volo, IL 60073

800.999.4660 USA Canada
800.889.5242 Technical Support
www.donjohnston.com

DON JOHNSTON

International Standard Book Number
ISBN 1-58702-368-7

Contents

Chapter 1

How Old Is That Kid?

Mrs. Chamberlain woke up and looked at her clock. It was 5 o'clock in the morning. She woke up every morning at this time when the streetcars started to rumble past her window. She was used to the noise because her house was just one block from the main streetcar station in Philadelphia. It was 1942.

But on this morning, Mrs. Chamberlain heard a new sound. "Something is wrong!" she thought.

She got out of bed. Her six daughters slept in one room and her three sons slept in another room. Mrs. Chamberlain looked in the boys' room. There were only two heads in the bed.

"Where's my baby?" she cried.

She ran to the window, opened the curtain and looked out.

There he was. Wilt was down there in the street. He was helping the milkman to pick up the crates of empty milk bottles from the houses along the block.

Mrs. Chamberlain ran downstairs. She rushed out onto the porch.

"What's my baby doing out here at 5 o'clock in the morning?" she hollered at the milkman. "Don't you know that it's wrong to make a little boy work like that?"

"But, Mama," said Wilt. "He gives me a nickel every morning!"

Wilt liked to do little jobs for people. He was always finding ways to make a little money.

"Come back to bed, son," she told him.

She turned to the milkman.

"Don't you ever try that again," she shouted. "Do your own work!"

The milkman just stood there. "Sorry, lady," he said. "I thought your boy was 12 years old!"

"12 years old!" Wilt's mother shouted. "He's only six!"

"You're kidding!" said the milkman. "He's as tall as *my* boys. And they're teenagers! That little baby of yours must be over five feet tall," he said.

The milkman was just like everyone else. No one could believe that a six-year-old boy could be so tall.

Wilt would not stop growing. Six years later, at the age of 12, he was 6 feet 3 inches tall. Wilt's older brother was also tall, but not as tall as his baby brother Wilt!

The Chamberlain children spent the summer out in the country. They went to stay on their uncle's farm. Wilt liked everything about the farm except one thing. Bugs! The bugs went crazy biting Wilt. He had scars and sores all over his legs!

Chapter 2

Throw Me the Ball!

Bettmann/CORBIS

In 1950, Wilt was 14 years old, but he was still in junior high school. He had been held back for a year in grade school because he was very sick and missed six months of school.

But now Wilt was feeling great. He had four friends, named Vince, Howard, Tommy, and Marty. They ran everywhere together. Wilt loved to run. He never walked. He ran in all the races at school, and he was fast.

One day, his friends came over to his house.

"Hey, Wilt," they said. "Come and shoot some hoops with us at the playground!"

Wilt didn't want to shoot hoops. His sport was track. He didn't think much about basketball.

Vince started to tease him. "Why do you love running so much?" Vince asked Wilt. "You can't make any money by running."

"That's OK," said Wilt. "You can't make any money by playing basketball! Look at you. You're black. They won't let you play in the NBA."

"Vince could play for the Harlem Globetrotters!" said Marty. "They're all black."

"The Globetrotters are the best team in the world!" said Tommy. "But they aren't allowed to play in the NBA!"

Wilt couldn't argue with that.

"Who says that a black man can't play in the NBA?" asked Vince. "Wait here!" he said.

Vince ran inside Wilt's house, and came back out with a newspaper.

"Read this!" said Vince.

The headline said, "CHUCK COOPER TO PLAY IN THE PROS."

Wilt read the story. It said that Chuck Cooper was the first black man to play in the NBA.

Vince slapped Wilt on the arm. "Do you still say that a black kid can't make money in basketball?" asked Vince.

"I didn't mean that," said Wilt. "I meant that *you* couldn't do it. I didn't say that *I* couldn't do it!"

Pretty soon, Wilt was playing basketball every day with his friends. They all joined the junior high school team.

At first, some of the kids didn't think that Wilt was so great. His long legs didn't look strong enough for basketball. And Wilt didn't fight for the ball on the court. He just wanted to have fun. He talked big with his friends, but he never pushed other kids around. Instead, the other kids pushed *him* around!

"Wilt is tall, but I bet that he won't ever make it to the pros," one kid told the coach. "He's not strong enough, and he's not tough enough."

But the coach could see that Wilt was more than tall. The coach could see that Wilt was also fast, and he was a great jumper. Maybe Wilt wasn't mean, but he played hard and he practiced hard.

The coach was right. Pretty soon, everyone was coming to the games to watch Wilt.

Wilt liked basketball. He liked running fast up and down the court. He liked to jump high and grab the ball out of the air. He liked to work on shooting and dribbling the ball.

Pretty soon, Wilt was also playing center on the team at the YMCA. At the Y, the other players weren't junior high school kids like Wilt. They were college players. But they wanted Wilt on their team.

They needed someone to play center.
They needed someone to grab the
rebounds and make hook shots
and jump shots and lay-ups. Pretty
soon, that team had won the national
championship of the YMCA.

Chapter 3

The Dipper

By the end of junior high school, Wilt was 6 feet 7 inches tall. When high school started three months later, he would be 6 feet 11 inches tall! Wilt grew four inches in just three months!

Wilt had to choose a high school. The best basketball teams in Philadelphia were at Catholic high schools. Wilt's family wasn't Catholic, but the coaches at two of the Catholic high schools wanted Wilt to go to their schools.

"I want your son to play for our team," one of the coaches told Mr. Chamberlain. "He can get a scholarship and come to our school for free."

"That sounds good," said Wilt's mother.

"And we'll give Wilt money for the streetcar and for lunch every day," said the coach.

"That sounds good!" said Wilt.

"I'll talk it over with my son and my family," Wilt's father told the coach. "Then, we'll let you know."

Later, Wilt said to his parents,
"I want to go to public school. I want
to be with my friends. I want to go
to Overbrook High School with Vince
and Howard and Tommy and Marty."

"Son, it's up to you," said his
parents. "You can go wherever you
want to go."

When Wilt walked down the hall
at Overbrook High, he heard the
students call out "Hey, Dipper!"
He liked the nickname because his
friends had made it up.

They had been playing basketball in the basement of an old house. There were pipes just below the ceiling and Wilt almost hit his head on a pipe during a game.

"Hey, Wilt! You better dip your head when you go under that pipe," his friends told him. Pretty soon, everyone was calling him "Dippy," and "Dipper," and "Big Dipper."

Before long, Wilt and his friends were all playing basketball for Overbrook.

Vince, Howard, Tommy, Marty, and Wilt were the five players who started every game. Their team won the public school championship every year.

In three years, they won 58 games and lost only three games.

Wilt was smashing the high school records. No one could stop him.

A high school basketball game is only 32 minutes long, but Wilt could score 40 or 50 points in a game. In one game, he scored 90 points!

The only team that could beat Overbrook was West Catholic High School. Before Wilt came along, the Catholic high schools had always won the city championship.

When Wilt was in the tenth grade, Overbrook High won the public school championship, but West Catholic won the city championship. How did they stop Wilt? Four of the West Catholic players ganged up on Wilt for the whole game! They were all over him.

The West Catholic players didn't pay any attention to the other players on the Overbrook team, so Wilt only scored 29 points, and West Catholic won.

The next year, Wilt fought back. He was only a junior, but he wasn't going to let other players push him around anymore. In that season, Overbrook High won all 20 games. They won both the public school and the city championships. The next year, they won both championships again!

After Wilt's last championship game, the other kids from Overbrook tried to pick him up on their shoulders and carry him off the court, but they couldn't do it because he was too big!

Wilt was the star at Overbrook High School, but he wasn't the most popular player. The other kids cheered more for Marty than they cheered for Wilt. Marty was smaller than Wilt, but Marty had more flash. Wilt felt trapped in his big body. He was a little jealous of Marty.

Chapter 4

Watch that Kid!

One day, two men came to a game at Overbrook High School. One man was a reporter. The other man was a coach from a college in Philadelphia.

"Watch that Wilt Chamberlain kid!" the reporter told the coach. "He's over seven feet tall now, but he isn't clumsy. You're going to like the way he moves."

The coach watched the game for a while. Then he told the reporter, "You're right. A lot of tall guys aren't good players. They only win because they're tall. But this Wilt kid is tall and fast. He has good moves," the coach continued. "It looks to me like he's a smart player."

"What do you mean?" asked the reporter

"Wilt can do it all," replied the coach. "He has a good jump shot. He can dunk the ball. He grabs all the rebounds and he can block shots."

The reporter watched Wilt for a while and then said, "He doesn't even look tired! He looks like he could play all day."

They watched Marty take a shot. It was a bad shot, so Wilt jumped up and steered it into the basket.

The coach laughed. "When Wilt stands below the basket and reaches up, his hand is only six inches from the rim. He's all legs! He looks like he's standing on stilts!" the coach said.

"That's a great nickname," said the reporter. "We'll call him Wilt the Stilt!"

Pretty soon the newspapers were all talking about Wilt the Stilt.

Wilt didn't like the name.

"It makes me sound like some kind of freak," he told his friends. "Don't call me Wilt the Stilt. Call me Dipper, or just call me Wilt!"

Wilt only had one problem on the basketball court. The problem was his socks. They kept sliding down to his ankles. It didn't look cool.

The other kids could see all the nasty scars and bug bites on his legs. The scars hurt when other players banged into him. But Wilt didn't have enough money to buy better socks.

So Wilt was always picking up rubber bands off the street to hold his socks up. In a game, he always kept an extra rubber band on his wrist. Even after he got to the pros, he still wore a rubber band on his wrist. It reminded him of the old days when he didn't have the money for better socks!

Chapter 5

Drafted!

One day, a man called Wilt to offer him a job. "I want you to come to the Catskill Mountains this summer," said the man. "I have a job for you at my resort."

A resort is a fancy hotel with beautiful land around it.   A resort may have a swimming pool and tennis courts and a golf course. There are many summer resorts in the Catskill Mountains in New York State.

Wilt was always looking for money. His parents worked all the time. His father was a handyman, and his mother cleaned houses. These jobs didn't pay much money, so the children were always trying to find ways to help out.

"What kind of a job is it?" asked Wilt.

"Well, it's really two jobs," said the man. "One job is being a bellhop."

Wilt laughed. "A bellhop? What's that?" he asked. "Some new kind of dance?"

The man laughed, too. "A bellhop carries suitcases for the people who stay at the resort," he explained. "And bellhops get *big* tips!"

"That sounds good," said Wilt. "What's the other job?"

"Playing basketball," said the man.

The resorts paid basketball players to teach the game and to play against other resorts in the summer. Most of the players were famous pros or college stars.

"I'm your man!" said Wilt.

So Wilt went to the Catskills for the summer. He was still in high school, but he played with the pros in the Catskills. And he beat them!

Two men were watching Wilt in the Catskills. One man was the coach of the Boston Celtics. His name was Red Auerbach. Red was a great coach, and the Celtics were the greatest team in the NBA.

Red came to the Catskills every summer. As soon as he saw Wilt play, Red wanted to draft him for the Celtics.

That meant that Wilt would agree to play for the Celtics after he finished college. But Red didn't tell Wilt about his plan. All he said was, "Hey, Wilt! Why don't you come to college in Boston. Boston has some great college basketball teams!"

Red hoped that Wilt would come to Boston because of a special NBA rule. The rule said that an NBA team could draft a player if the player went to college near the NBA team.

So if Wilt went to college in Boston, the Celtics could draft him! But Red was sneaky. He didn't tell Wilt about the rule.

Another man was even sneakier than Red Auerbach. This man's name was Eddie Gottlieb. Eddie owned an NBA team in Philadelphia called the Warriors. Eddie had a lot of power in the NBA, so he called a meeting of the team owners.

"Let's make a new rule," Eddie told the other owners. "This new rule will say that we can draft a player from any high school that is near our team. The player can go away to college, but after four years he will have to come back and play for us."

"You're crazy, Eddie," said the other owners. "Why would you want to draft a player if he can't play for you until four years later?"

Eddie just smiled to himself as the other owners agreed to the new rule.

Then Eddie told them, "You can call me crazy, but I'm drafting Wilt Chamberlain for the Philadelphia Warriors!"

Red Auerbach was angry, but he couldn't change the rule. He wasn't an owner. He was just a coach. And Wilt couldn't change the rule either.

Chapter 6

Why Kansas?

As Wilt finished high school, coaches from colleges all around the country started going after him. In the 12th grade, Wilt was spending almost every weekend flying somewhere to visit a college. He spent so much time at the airport that some people thought he worked there!

Near the end of high school, the telephone and the doorbell at the Chamberlain's house never stopped ringing.

Every day, the mailbox was filled with stacks of letters from colleges. Wilt even had dreams that the coaches were climbing through his window!

Wilt wanted to get away from his hometown and he wanted to go to a college where basketball was really popular. He wanted to be the star athlete of the school. And he wanted people to like him as much as they liked Marty!

After a lot of thinking and talking, Wilt finally chose the University of Kansas in Lawrence, Kansas.

But why Kansas? Why did Wilt pick the University of Kansas? Basketball was big in Kansas, but the University of Kansas did not have a great team, and Kansas could be a lonely place for a young black man. There were only a few other blacks at the University. At that time, a lot of the restaurants in Lawrence would not even serve food to a black person.

Later, Wilt made up a lot of reasons
about why he chose Kansas. Each
of those reasons had a little bit of truth
in it. But here is the *real* truth! Here
are the two biggest reasons why Wilt
went to Kansas.

One big reason was money! A lot
of coaches were offering Wilt money
if he would come to their college, but
the money had to be a secret.

The other big reason that Wilt went
to Kansas was because his mother
liked the idea.

The coach for the University of Kansas was a man named Phog Allen. Coach Allen flew to Philadelphia to see Mrs. Chamberlain. He spent a lot of time telling her what a good place Kansas would be for her baby!

Coach Allen thought that getting Wilt to join the team was like catching a fish. Allen was the fisherman, and Wilt was the fish! Coach Allen was putting a lot of money on the hook for bait.

College sports are run by the NCAA.
The NCAA had a rule about giving gifts
to players. The rule said that schools
couldn't give gifts to an athlete.
A college could give a scholarship
to a player to help pay for classes.
The college could pay for his room,
food, and things like laundry. It could
also give him a job so that he could
earn some money. But the college
could *not* just give him a pile of money
for free!

Many colleges cheated to get the best players. The University of Kansas found ways to give Wilt lots of money for playing basketball. They got people who had already graduated from the school to give him money. These people are called alumni. After each game, the alumni would give Wilt handfuls of $100 bills. One of the alumni gave Wilt a job selling cars. But Wilt didn't have to do any work at the car lot. He could just pretend that he was working there.

The coaches said, "Wilt, if you need something, just ask for it. Our alumni will take care of you."

Wilt thought about that for a moment. Then he smiled and said, "I want a Cadillac!"

So the alumni gave him a Cadillac.

The money was important to Wilt and his family. In some ways, the money made him feel good. He wanted to be rich. He wanted to own fast cars and buy a nice new home for his parents.

But secretly, Wilt felt a little bad about the money. He felt as if the alumni were buying him. And he felt as if the fans expected him to win the games all by himself. It was a lonely feeling.

Chapter 7

Ways to Stop Wilt

At the University of Kansas, Coach Allen put a lot of pressure on Wilt. The coach told the reporters, "We will never lose with Wilt Chamberlain on our team! We don't really need anyone else."

Of course, that wasn't true. It was the wrong thing to say. Now, if the team lost, people could blame it all on Wilt.

In those days, a college student couldn't play on the varsity team during his freshman year.

The varsity team usually has the school's best players, but Wilt had to wait a year to play varsity, even though he was the best player for miles around. When Coach Allen had the freshman team play against the varsity team, the freshman team won the game and Wilt scored 42 points.

In the meantime, the NCAA made new rules to make the game harder for Wilt. One rule was about "offensive goaltending." When a team has the ball, that team is called the offense. The other team is called the defense.

When Wilt's team was on offense, he would watch his teammates take a shot. If Wilt saw that the ball was going to miss the basket, he would jump up and steer the ball into the basket! The NCAA called that "offensive goaltending." The new rule said that Wilt wasn't allowed to do this anymore.

Wilt also had a special way of getting points on free throws. First, he would shoot the ball from the free throw line. Then, he would jump toward the basket.

If he missed the free throw, he would grab the ball and dunk it! Soon the NCAA made another new rule to stop him from doing that, too. The new rule said that a player could not cross the free throw line until *after* the ball had reached the basket.

But the new rules didn't stop Wilt. In Wilt's first game, he broke two Kansas records. He scored 52 points in one game, and he grabbed 31 rebounds.

His team won 12 games in a row before any other team could beat them. That team won by having three guys gang up on Wilt for the whole game. It was just like in high school!

Then other teams started ganging up on Wilt. And they got really rough with him. They stopped him by banging into his long legs and pushing their elbows into his face. The referees let the other teams do those things, even though it was against the rules.

Bettmann/CORBIS

When a player breaks a rule, the referee is supposed to call a foul. But the refs didn't call many fouls. They acted like it was OK for the other players to bash into Wilt because he was so big!

Kansas still won 21 games in that season and lost only two games. Then the team played in the tournament for the NCAA national championship, and they went all the way to the final game.

In the final game, Kansas would be playing against a great team from North Carolina that had not been beaten all season long.

Carolina had a great coach named Frank McGuire. Coach McGuire was smart. He told his players, "There is only one way that we can beat Kansas. Forget about the other Kansas players. They are not great shooters. Our whole team is going to play defense against Wilt Chamberlain!"

Chapter 8

Showdown at the NCAA

Wilt watches as a player from the North Carolina
team scores a goal.

It was a great championship game. Carolina slowed Wilt down, but they could not stop him all the time. By the end of the game, the score was tied at 46-46, so the teams had to keep playing in overtime. It was the first time that an NCAA championship game had ever gone into overtime.

In the overtime period, both teams were careful. Carolina scored on a lay-up. Then Wilt hit a jump shot and the score was tied again at 48-48. The first overtime period ended. The game went into a second overtime!

Both teams felt the pressure. All of the players were nervous. Both teams missed their shots. Then Wilt got into a scramble for a loose ball with a player from Carolina. All the players on both teams ran out on the court and started pushing and shoving each other. The referees ordered them to go back to their benches.

Now the game went into a third overtime period! Carolina made a two-point shot. Then a Kansas player fouled a Carolina player, which gave the Carolina player two free throws.

The Carolina player made the two free throws and put his team ahead, 52-48.

Then Wilt got the ball. He shot the ball, made a basket for two points, and was fouled. The refs let him have one free throw, and he made it! The score was 52-51. Now Kansas was just one point behind!

A Kansas player got fouled. He made his first free throw, but he missed his second one. Now the score was tied again at 52-52.

Then *another* Kansas player was fouled! He made one free throw, and Kansas was ahead by one point!

Carolina got the ball. A Carolina player was fouled, and he made two free throws. Now Carolina was ahead by one point, 54-53!

There were only six seconds left in the overtime period. A Kansas player tried to pass the ball to Wilt, but a Carolina player batted it away. The game was over. Kansas had lost by one point.

It was one of the best games in the history of the NCAA, but Wilt was upset that his team had lost. He felt terrible. For the rest of his life, he thought about that game. But Wilt should have been proud, because without him the team wouldn't even have come close to beating Carolina.

After the game, Coach McGuire from Carolina made fun of Wilt. He said, "It was like the story of Jack and the beanstalk. We chopped down the beanstalk."

Later, Coach McGuire was sorry for those words. He knew that Wilt could be one of the greatest players who ever lived. He also knew that basketball was a game for teams. Coach Allen had been wrong. One lonely great player is never enough to win in a team sport. This was a hard lesson for Wilt to learn, too. Wilt played for Kansas for one more year, but it wasn't a good year. The other Kansas players were not as good as before, and other teams kept ganging up on Wilt.

Players kept fouling Wilt, but the
referees didn't pay any attention.
One player hit Wilt with his knee
on purpose. Wilt was hurt, but he had
to keep playing. The other teams did
plenty of other dirty things to stop him.
The fans at other schools even shouted
racist names at him because he was
black.

After that season, Wilt quit college.
He hated college basketball. He wanted
to join the NBA and play in the pros.
He wanted to make more money
so that his parents could stop working.

The NBA told Wilt that he had to wait one more year before he could play in the pros, so Wilt decided to join the Harlem Globetrotters. The Globetrotters played games all over the world. They made the whole world love basketball. The Globetrotters weren't all about winning. They were great basketball players, but the most important thing about their game was giving the fans a good time.

Wilt loved the Globetrotters. He loved how they joked around and did fancy tricks with the basketball.

Wilt loved the Globetrotters so much that he came back and played for them almost every summer, even when he was an NBA star.

Chapter 9

The Rookie Who Changed the NBA

Basketball Hall of Fame, Springfield, MA

In 1959, Wilt Chamberlain joined the Philadelphia Warriors. He made them into a winning team. Then, in 1962, Wilt and the team moved to the west coast and became the San Francisco Warriors. In 1965, Wilt went back to his hometown to play for the Philadelphia 76ers.

In the NBA, Wilt was great on offense and great on defense. In college, he had started lifting weights to make his upper body stronger. In the NBA, no one could stop him. They could only slow him down.

Basketball Hall of Fame, Springfield, MA

There has never been a center who could do all the things that Wilt Chamberlain could do. Everyone knows that he could score, but he could also rebound and dribble, and he could pass the ball. He could block shots like a man standing on a ladder. And night after night, he played every minute of every game.

Of course, Wilt was named Rookie of the Year in 1959. In his first year, he was also the MVP, or most valuable player, of the NBA.

Wilt brought thousands of new fans to the NBA. Everybody wanted to see him play. So Wilt asked for more money than other players were getting, and he got it. Why? Because he was making the NBA owners rich! Wilt did a favor for the other players. He led the way for other basketball stars to get rich.

Wilt broke more NBA records than any other player has ever broken.

Here are a few of his records:

- He scored over 50 points per game for a whole season. He led the NBA in scoring for seven years in a row.

- He scored 35 baskets in a row without missing. He scored 28 free throw points in one game.

- He got 55 rebounds in one game. For 11 seasons, he led the NBA in rebounds. For 13 seasons, he got more than 1000 rebounds each season.

- For 47 games in a row, he played every minute of every game. In his NBA career, he played 47,859 minutes.

After Wilt's rookie year, the NBA tried to make the game even harder for him. The NBA made new rules to keep Wilt away from the basket. One rule said that a player couldn't stay inside the free throw lane for more than three seconds at a time. They also made the free throw lane wider to keep Wilt farther away from the basket. But Wilt still ruled the NBA!

Basketball Hall of Fame, Springfield, MA

Did Wilt have any weaknesses? Yes. In high school and college, he was good at shooting free throws, but when he got to the NBA, he lost this skill. He could make free throws in practice, but he missed a lot of them in games. Wilt never could understand what was wrong.

So Wilt found a new way to shoot his free throws. He would run up to the free throw line, then jump all the way to the basket and dunk the ball! You can probably guess what happened. The NBA changed its rules again.

They said that Wilt had to stay behind the free throw line until the ball hit the basket. No more slam-dunking free throws!

It's a problem if you can't make free throws in the NBA. If you are bad at free throws, the other teams will try to foul you. Then if you miss your free throw, they will grab the rebound. That's what happened to Wilt. Other teams would chase him all over the court just so they could foul him! Wilt was a giant, but he took a lot of bashing in the NBA.

Chapter 10

The Gentle Giant

Bettmann/CORBIS

Wilt and his teammates win the NBA championship in 1967.

For 14 years, Wilt Chamberlain was the most powerful player in the NBA. But in those same years, the Boston Celtics were the best team. Red Auerbach was their coach. Almost every year, Red coached the Celtics to the championship. In 1967, Wilt and the 76ers finally took the championship away from the Celtics. Many basketball fans say that those 76ers were the greatest basketball team of all time.

The next year, the 76ers played another great season, but they lost to the Celtics in the playoffs.

After that, the team broke up. In 1968, Wilt was traded to the Los Angeles Lakers. In the season of 1971-1972, Wilt and the Lakers won 33 games in a row. They also won the championship.

Some people said that Wilt was like the giant "Goliath" in the Bible. But this wasn't fair to Wilt, because Goliath was a cruel giant, and Wilt was gentle. He didn't like to foul other players. In 14 years in the NBA, Wilt never fouled out of a game. But that was also a problem for him.

Basketball Hall of Fame, Springfield, MA

Why? Because the other teams could be rough on Wilt all night, and the referees would hardly ever call a foul against them. This was because Wilt was so much bigger than the other players.

Wilt was not *always* gentle. He was not afraid of fights. He broke up fights between other players. If Wilt didn't like the way that someone on the other team was acting, he could just pick the man up like a toothpick and carry him off the court!

Wilt set one record that may never be broken. It happened in a game against the New York Knicks on March 2, 1962. That was the night when Wilt scored 100 points in a single game.

There have been many great basketball stars since Wilt left the NBA in 1973. Some of these stars have even broken some of Wilt's records.

But no one has come close to breaking the three records that he set in the 1961-62 season:

- Scoring the most points in one game: 100 points

- Scoring the most points in one season: 4,029 points

- Scoring an average of 50 points a game for a whole season

Basketball Hall of Fame, Springfield, MA

Wilt standing next to his picture at the Basketball Hall of Fame.

In 1978, Wilt Chamberlain was chosen for the Basketball Hall of Fame. Some players say that Wilt was just one of the biggest and strongest players in basketball, but many famous players say that he was the greatest basketball player in history. And they all agree that Wilt Chamberlain changed the sport of basketball forever.

The End

Bibliography

Selected Sources

Chamberlain, Wilt, and Shaw, David. *Wilt: Just like any other 7-foot black millionaire who lives next door.* New York: Macmillan Publishing Company, Inc., 1973.

Frankl, Ron. *Wilt Chamberlain.* Introduction by Chuck Daly. New York: Chelsea House Publishers, 1994.

Hickok, Ralph. *A Who's Who of Sports Champions: Their Stories & Records.* New York: Houghton Mifflin Company, 1995.

Libby, Bill. Goliath: *The Wilt Chamberlain Story.* New York: Dodd, Mead & Co., 1977.

Web Sites

nba.com, "Wilt Chamberlain." *http://www.nba.com/history/chamberlain_bio.html*

"The official web site of Wilt Chamberlain," maintained by Wilt Chamberlain's estate. *http://www.wiltchamberlain.com*

About the Start-to-Finish Writer

Alan Venable was born in Pittsburgh, Pennsylvania, in 1944 and has lived and traveled in various parts of America, Africa, and Asia. In addition to his books in the Start-to-Finish series, he has written several books of fiction for children, school curricular texts, and plays and novels for adults. He lives in San Francisco where he enjoys walking the hills, exploring new music, and learning new languages.

About the Reader

Bernard Mixon is a professional actor who performs on the stage, in films, and in many television shows and commercials. On stage, Bernard has played the role of Julius Caesar at the Black Ensemble Theatre and the role of the lion in the popular play, *The Wiz.* You may have seen Bernard as Magic Sam in the television series, *America's Most Wanted,* or as Ross Thomas in *The Mary Thomas Story.*

Bernard has also worked for the Chicago Historical Society and Urban Gateways , and played the roles of many famous people from history.

For the past ten years, Bernard has been singing jazz, pop, country and gospel music with a band called *The Moods.* When he performs with this group, he also plays the harmonica, drums and other kinds of percussion instruments.

A Note from the Start-to-Finish Editors

You will notice that Start-to-Finish Books look different from other high-low readers and chapter books. The text layout of this book coordinates with the other media components (CD and audiocassette) of the Start-to-Finish series.

The text in the book matches, line-for-line and page-for-page, the text shown on the computer screen, enabling readers to follow along easily in the book. Each page ends in a complete sentence so that the student can either practice the page (repeat reading) or turn the page to continue with the story. If the next sentence cannot fit on the page in its entirety, it has been shifted to the next page. For this reason, the sentence at the top of a page may not be indented, signaling that it is part of the paragraph from the preceding page.

Words are not hyphenated at the ends of lines. This sometimes creates extra space at the end of a line, but eliminates confusion for the struggling reader.